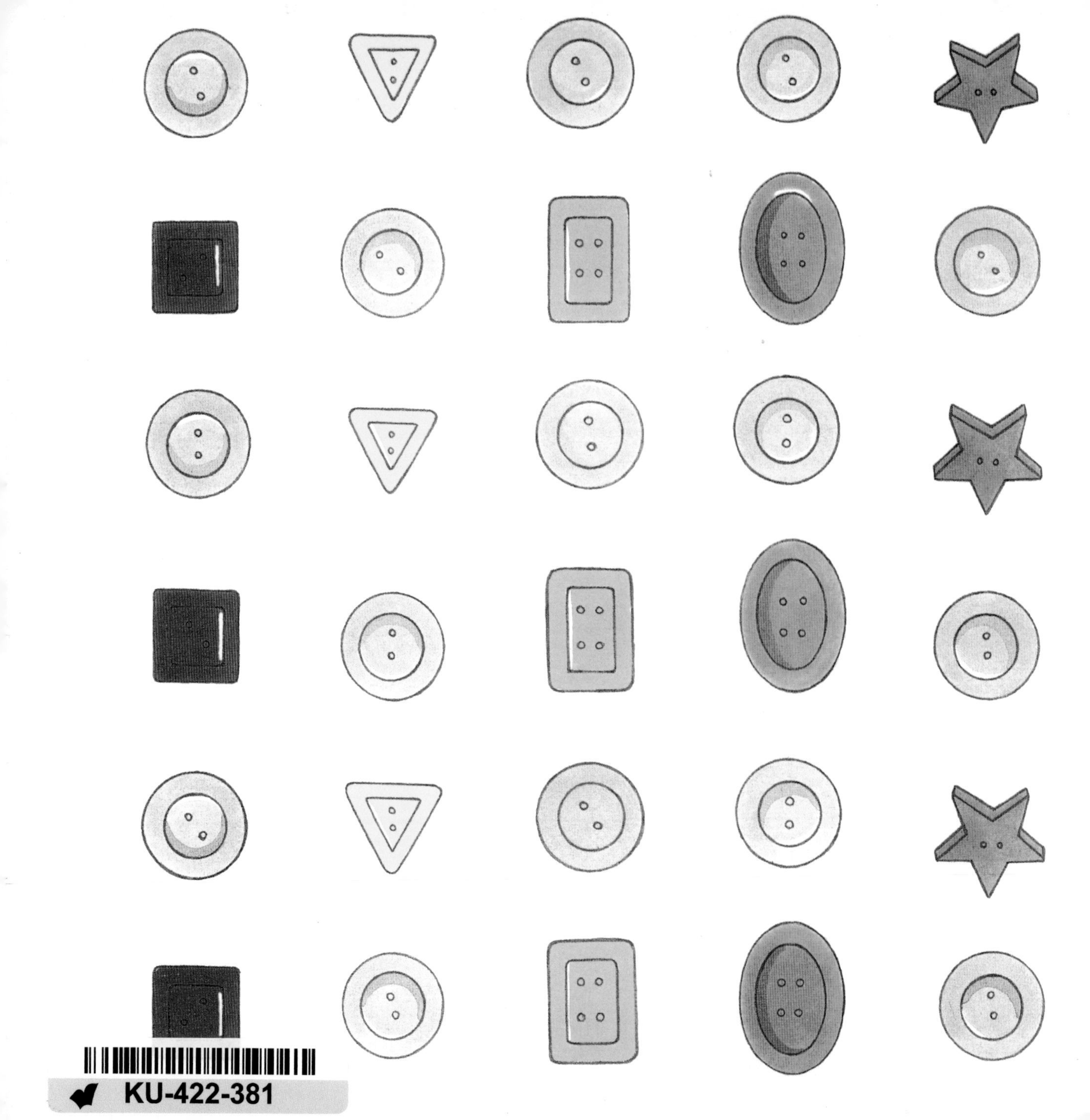

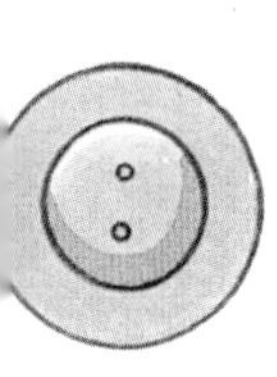

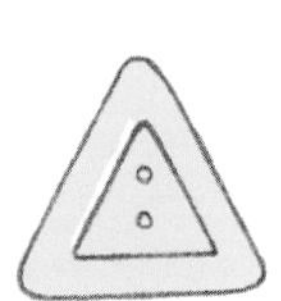

BIG BEAR
AND THE BLUE BUTTON

Written by Stephanie Laslett
Illustrated by John Blackman

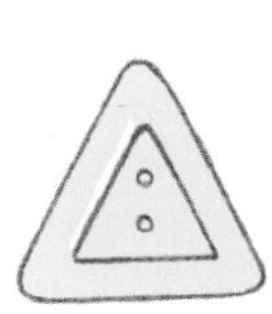
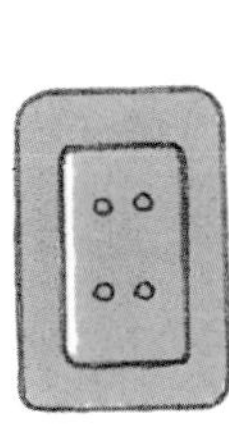

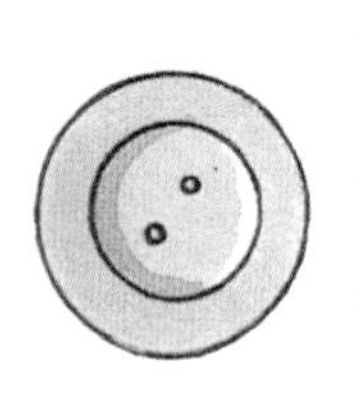

Wake up Big Bear!
Wake up Morris Mouse!

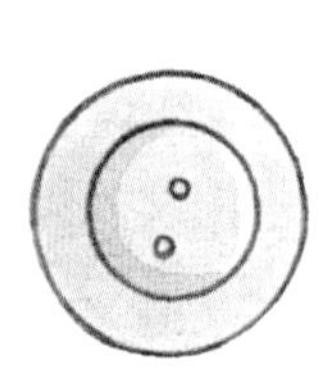

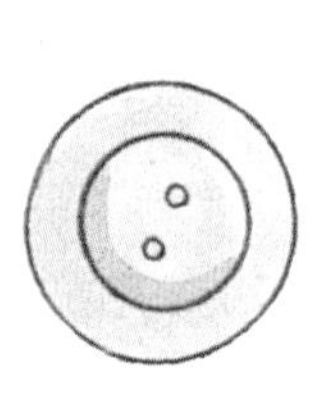

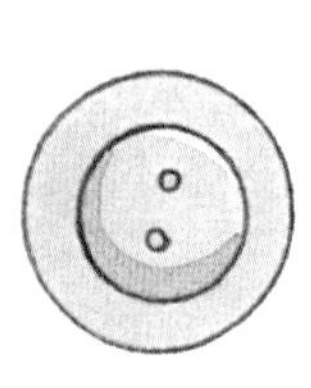

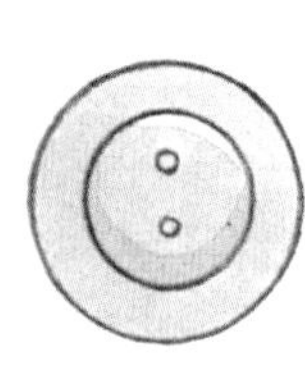

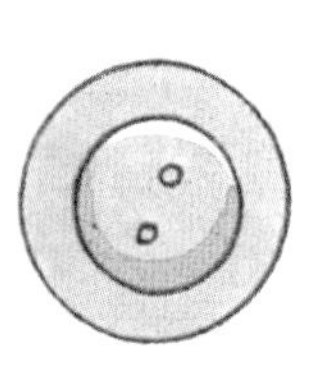

Time to get up.

Time to do our exercises.

Stretch up high.

Bend down low.

What has Big
Bear found?
Is this your
round blue
button?

No. My buttons are **red** and shaped like a **square**.

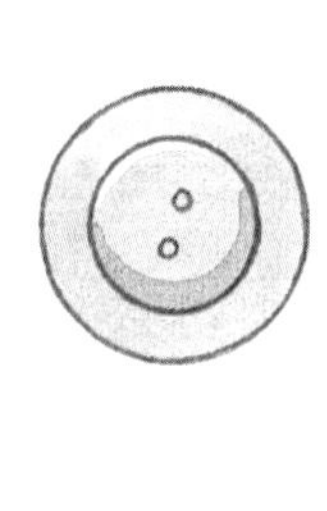

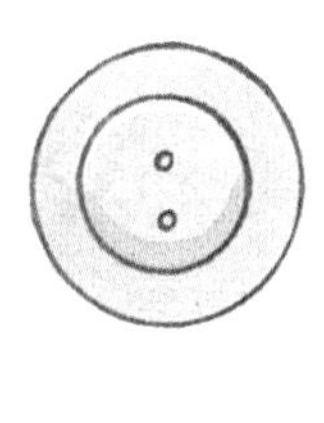

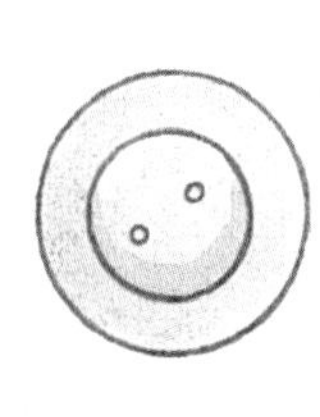

Hello, Percy Pig. Is this your **round blue** button?

No. My buttons are **yellow** and shaped like a **triangle**.

Boris Badger has arrived.
Is this your round **blue button**?
No. My buttons
are **green** and
shaped like a
rectangle.

There's Olive Owl
walking past.

Is this your **round blue** button Olive?

No. My buttons are **pink** and shaped like an **oval**.

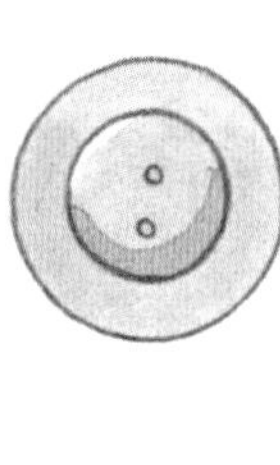

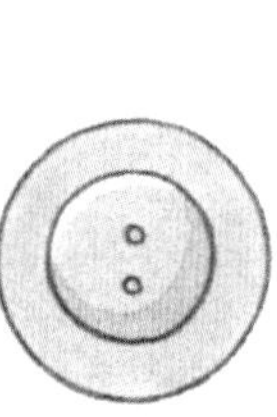

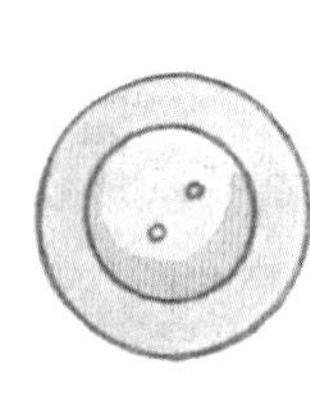

Has this **round blue** button popped off your bag?

No. My bag has buttons which are **purple** and shaped like **stars**.

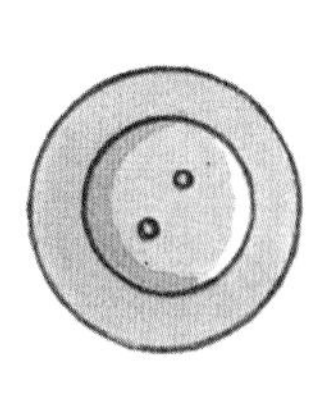
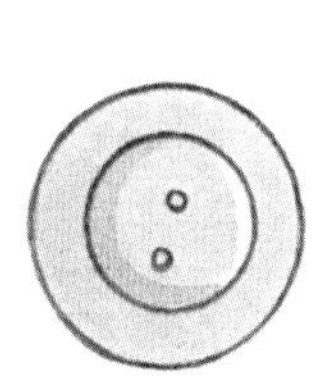
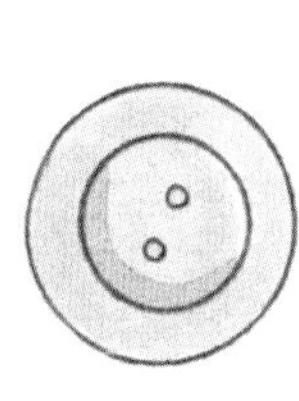
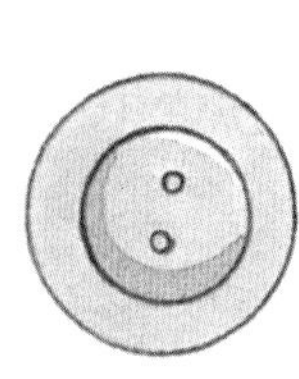
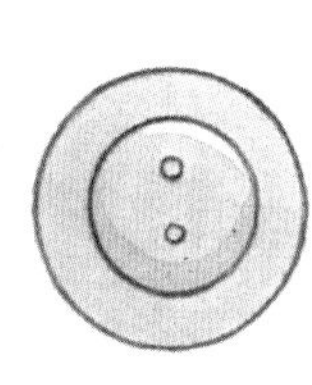
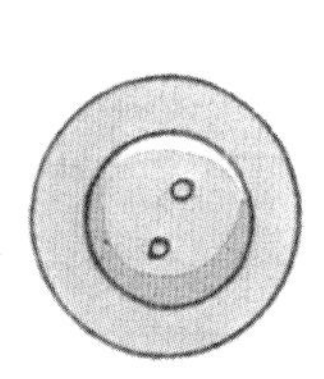

Whose is this
round blue button?

Hoo, hoo, hoo!
hoots Olive Owl.
Your trousers
have **round**
blue buttons.

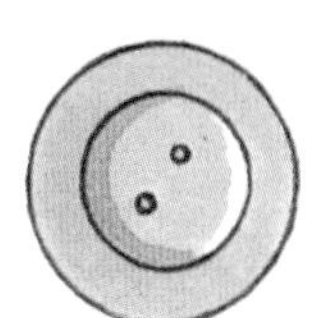
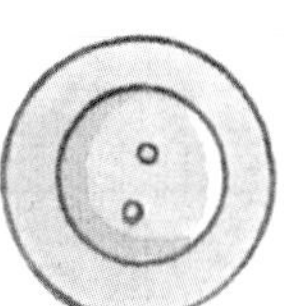

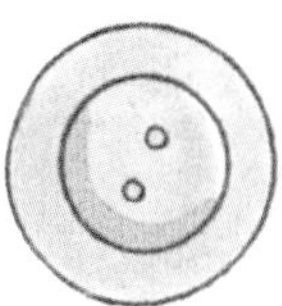
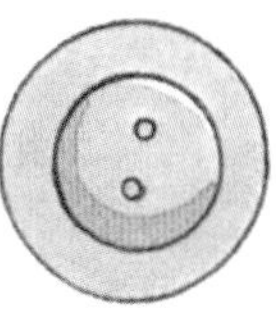
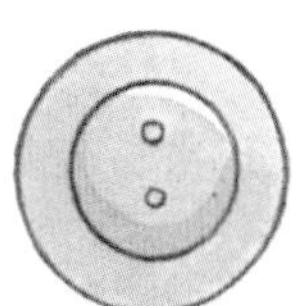
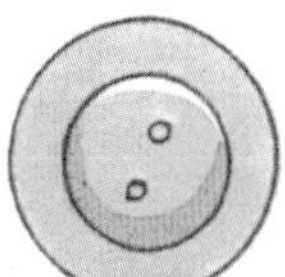

It is *your* button Big Bear.

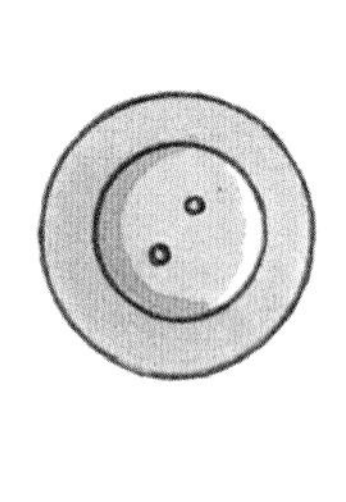
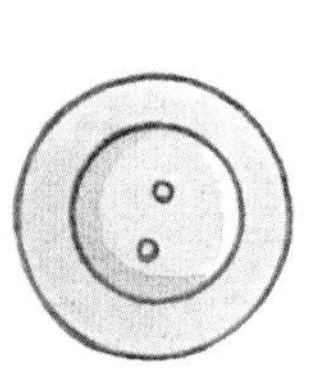
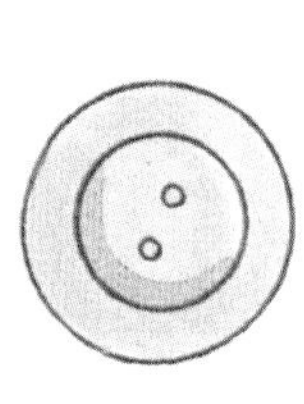
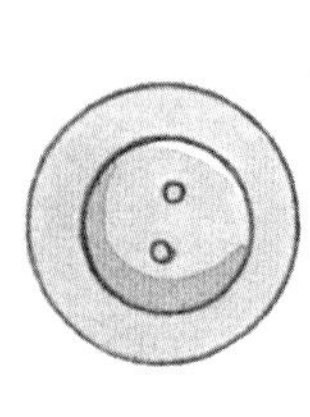
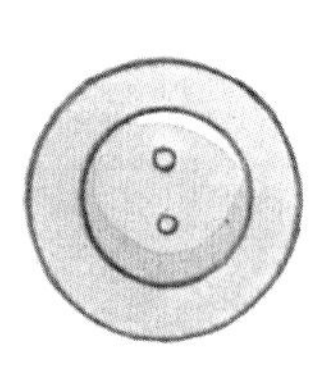
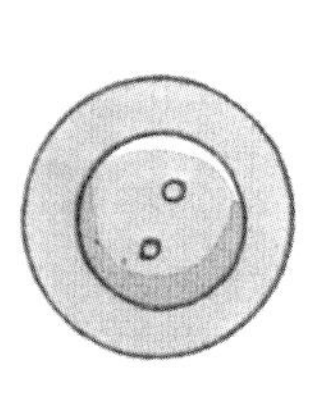

It popped off when you bent down to touch your toes!

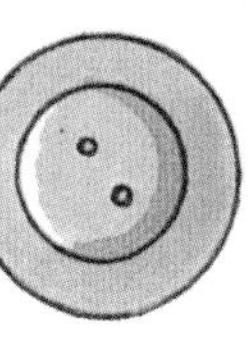
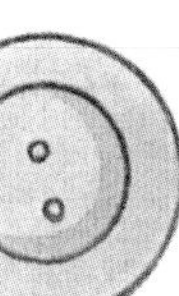
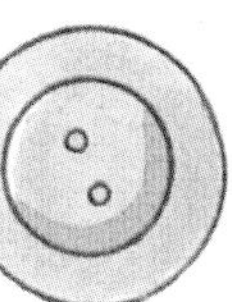
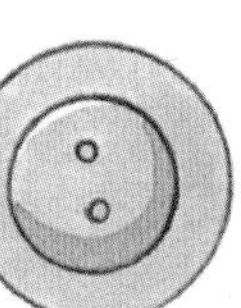
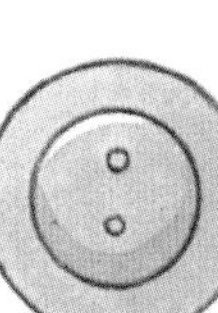
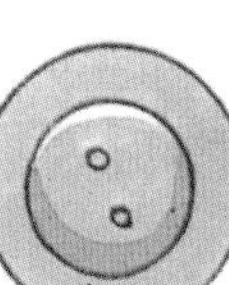

Now we all have our buttons!

Yellow Triangle
Green Rectangle
Pink Oval
Purple Star

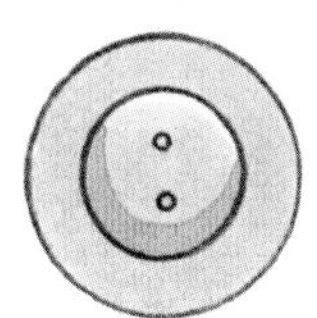

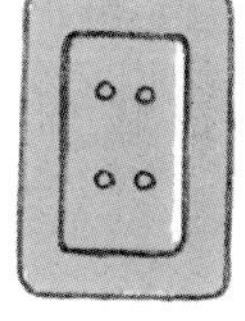

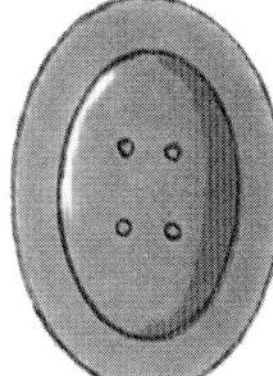

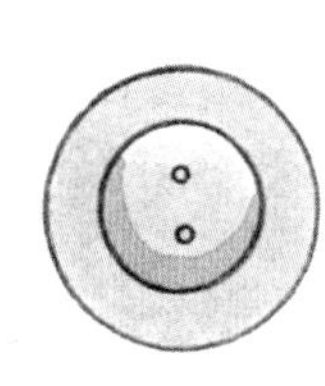
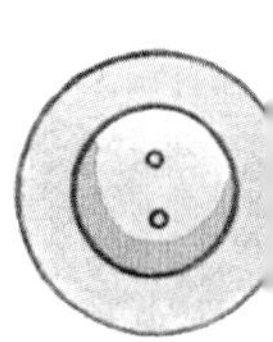
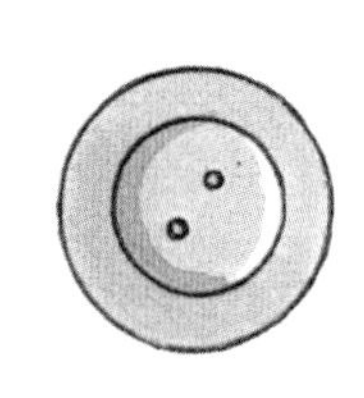

A PARRAGON BOOK

Published by Parragon Books,
Unit 13-17, Avonbridge Trading Estate,
Atlantic Road, Avonmouth, Bristol BS 11 9QD.

Produced by The Templar Company plc,
Pippbrook Mill, London Road, Dorking, Surrey RH4 1JE.

Designed by Janie Louise Hunt

Printed and bound in Italy

ISBN 0-75250-968-3

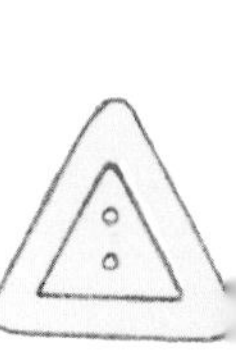
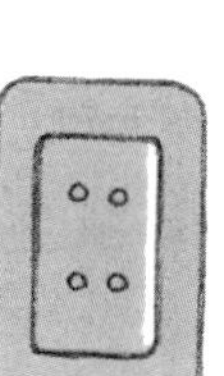
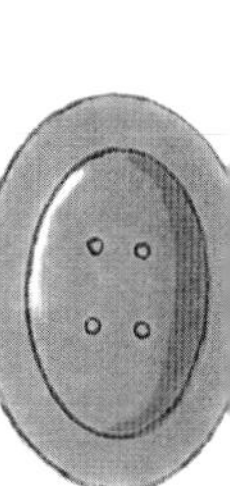
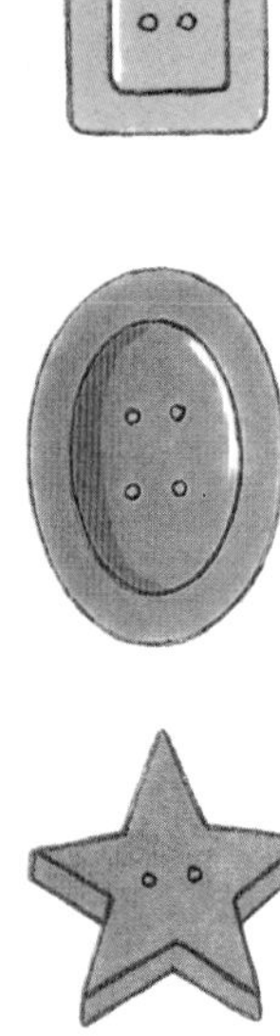

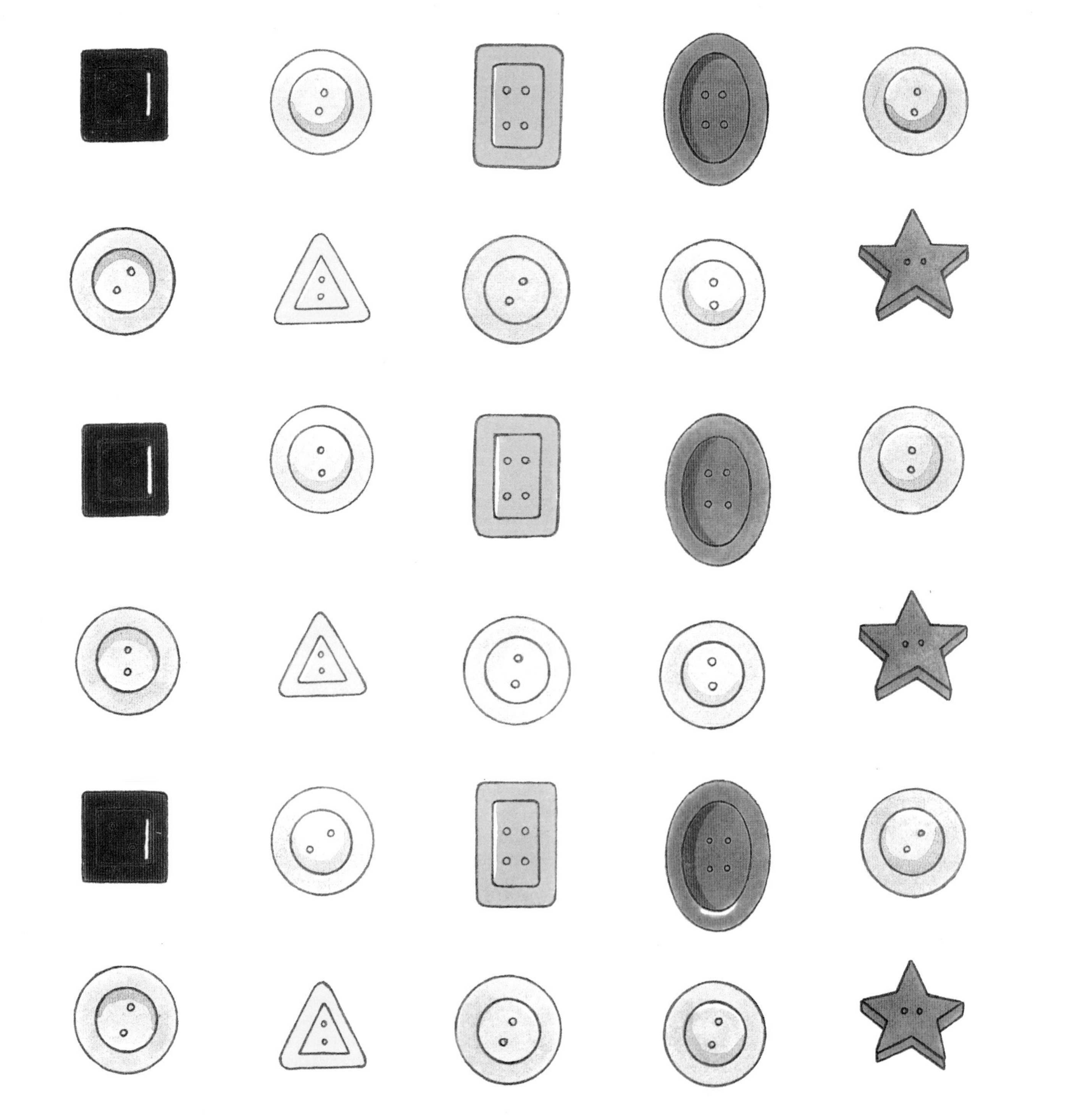